Too Many Chickens

For Carol Kerr and Cheryl Dinnin
who inspire big and little writers
P.B.
For Esperança
B.S.

Kids Can Press Ltd. acknowledges with appreciation the assistance of the Canada Council and the Ontario Arts Council in the production of this book.

Canadian Cataloguing in Publication Data

Bourgeois, Paulette
    Too many chickens

ISBN 0-921103-95-6 (bound)
ISBN 1-55074-067-9 (pbk.)

I. Slavin, Bill.   II. Title.

PS8553.087T66   1990   jC813'.54   C89-090557-6
PZ7.B67T0   1990

Kids Can Press Ltd.,
585½ Bloor Street West,
Toronto, Ontario, Canada M6G 1K5

Book design by N.R. Jackson
Printed and bound in Hong Kong

PA 92 0 9 8 7 6 5 4 3 2 1

TOO MANY CHICKENS

Written by Paulette Bourgeois
Illustrated by Bill Slavin

KIDS CAN PRESS LTD.
Toronto

Mrs. Kerr's class wiggled and squiggled and giggled. The farmer had brought the eggs — a dozen eggs that would soon be chicks. They were oval and speckled and smelled like a chicken coop.

Michael Alexander wrinkled his nose. Mrs. Kerr rolled her eyes and asked the farmer, politely, to put the eggs in the incubator.

The class took good care of the eggs. They turned them and checked them. They worried about them at night.

And then, on the twenty-first day, a crack marbled the surface of an egg. The crack widened.

"Rat, tat, tat," needled the beak.

For the very first time, Mrs. Kerr's class was still. The eggs opened, one by one, like ice cracking in the spring.

All the chicks hatched.
They were the colour of
sweet butter and as soft as
cotton balls.

The principal came to see the chicks. The caretaker came to see the chicks. Even the grade sixes came to see the chicks.

"Aren't they cute?" they cooed. The chicks went "Peep!" and tried to hop over the edge of the brooder.

On Monday, the farmer was supposed to come and get the chicks, but she never arrived. By Thursday, the chicks were big enough to jump. Mrs. Kerr was worried.

Every day they grew a little bigger. They were noisy and speckled and smelled like a chicken coop. They roosted on the science table and pecked under desks. They clawed at the carpet. They took baths in the sinks and shook their soggy feathers on the art supplies. They were always hungry. Mrs. Kerr kept a bag of seed in her desk.

The rooster found his crowing voice and the hens never stopped chattering.

"I CAN'T STAND THIS ANYMORE!"

screamed Michael Alexander when a chicken walked across his brand new notebook. "They are noisy and ugly and they stink!"

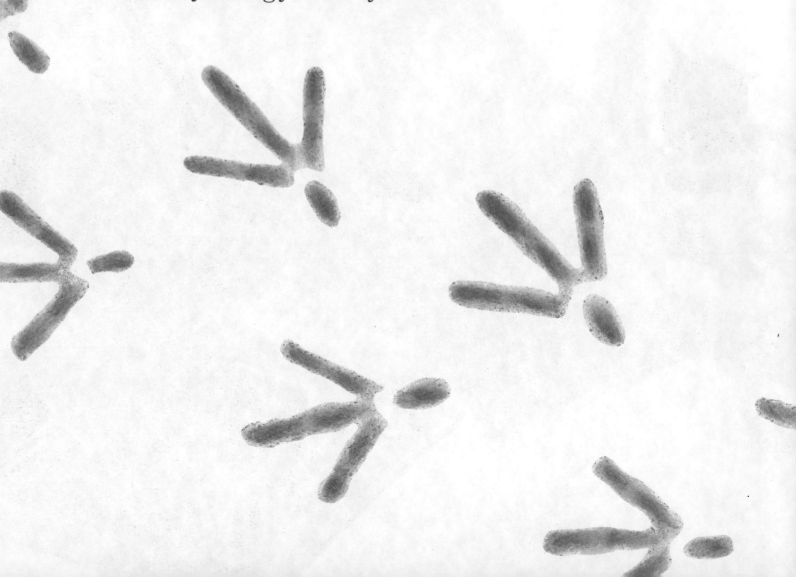

It was true. The chicks weren't cute anymore.
And they did smell. Nobody visited Room 17, not
even the caretaker.

Then the chicks started laying eggs.
   Michael Alexander painted a sign and Mrs. Kerr
taught the children how to reach under the
hens and gather eggs.

Finally, the farmer came. She was most apologetic. She already had so many chickens she forgot to pick up the chicks.

The farmer looked around Room 17 and grinned.

"These chickens look so happy," she said. "I can't bear to take them away."

Before Mrs. Kerr could interrupt, the farmer added, "Here's a little present for all you've done."

Michael Alexander shuddered. Mrs. Kerr rolled her eyes.

"Bunnies," said Mrs. Kerr. "How cute."

The rabbits had long white fur, pink eyes and crinkly wet noses.

The principal came to see the bunnies. The caretaker came to see the bunnies. Even the grade sixes came to see the bunnies.

Soon, there were four more bunnies. Mrs. Kerr had to build a bigger cage. She kept carrots and alfalfa in her desk.

Before long, there were sixteen bunnies. But Mrs. Kerr wasn't worried. Michael Alexander painted a new sign and Mrs. Kerr taught the class how to knit.

Soon, everyone was wearing an angora hat. Even the farmer. Why, she was so happy with her new hat that she gave Mrs. Kerr's class a present.

Michael Alexander gasped. Mrs. Kerr rolled
her eyes. There, outside the school, hunched
over the grass, was a great, big, old nanny goat.

"The old goat smells," said Michael Alexander.

"I know," said Mrs. Kerr.

"At least she eats the grass," said Michael Alexander.

"And I think the caretaker likes her," said Mrs. Kerr.

There was no way to get rid of the old goat. But Mrs. Kerr wasn't worried. Michael Alexander took out his paints. Mrs. Kerr kept apples in her desk and taught the children how to milk.

People liked the goat's milk. The caretaker bought two glasses every morning and said he'd never felt better.

Mrs. Kerr's class earned enough money from selling eggs and milk and hats to buy a small farm far away from the school. The caretaker decided he'd always wanted to live in the country. He took the chickens and the bunnies and the goat and went to live on the farm.

The children stopped milking and knitting and gathering the eggs. Michael Alexander had no more signs to make. Mrs. Kerr finally had time to teach what she was supposed to teach.

"We're going to learn about seeds," she announced.

And then, Mrs. Kerr pulled four bags of seeds from her desk drawer: Jack-in-the-Beanstalk Bean Seeds, Giant Pumpkin Seeds, Mile High Popping Corn Seeds and Bursting Bloom Tomato Seeds.

The children smirked. And Michael Alexander got out the paints.